THE
WINTER
GIFT

Deborah Turney Zagwyn

TRICYCLE PRESS * BERKELEY, CALIFORNIA

For Simon, who knows the joy and
burden of gifts handed down

A'SOALIN', by Paul Stookey, Tracy Batteast, and Elena Mezzetti
© 1963 (Renewed) Neworld Media Music Publishers
All rights administered by WB Music Corp.
All rights reserved. Used by permission.
Warner Bros. Publications U.S. INC.
Miami, FL 33014

Tricycle Press
P.O. Box 7123
Berkeley, California 94707

Book design by Tasha Hall

Library of Congress Cataloging-in-Publication Data
Zagwÿn, Deborah Turney.
     The winter gift / Deborah Turney Zagwÿn.
         p. cm.
     Summary: At Christmas, while she is moving
to an apartment, Gramma tries to sell the old family piano
but changes her mind when she sees how much her grand-
children love it and the memories it holds.
     ISBN 1-883672-93-7
     [1. Grandmothers—Fiction. 2. Christmas—Fiction.
3. Piano—Fiction. 4. Moving, Household—Fiction.] I. Title.
PZ7.Z245 Wi   2000   99-052823
[E]—dc21

First printing, 2000.
Printed in Hong Kong
1 2 3 4 5 6 7 — 04 03 02 01 00

*Hey ho,
nobody
home,*

*Meat nor
drink nor
money have
I none,*

*Yet shall we
be merry…*

—A'SOALIN'

It was almost Christmas and Gramma's house was not like Gramma's house at all. Outside it was the same as ever, same trees, same hillside tucked under the same frozen lake, same chickadees quarreling at the suet feeder. But inside Gramma's house there was not much to look at.

There were three empty boxes and a big brown piano with its bench—and that was all.

Gramma's house had always been full at Christmas—full of company, rich cooking smells, and lively music. Her tree was put up nice and early so that all the Christmas bobbles could be looked at and all the presents could be longed for well ahead of time. Gramma was not one to worry about a few pineneedles on her carpet. That is why Clee's family always had Christmas at Gramma's house.

But this year Gramma was moving. She had sold her house and much of her furniture. Clee's parents had driven her recipe books and photo albums and her ailing African violets to a new place on the other side of town.

Clee felt like Baby Bear in the story about the Three Bears.
"Who will dare to eat and sit and sleep in my Gramma's house?"
she fretted. She wished she could scare the new people away and
put back Gramma's bowls and chairs and beds.

So now Clee and her little brother Simon sat half on and half off the piano bench with Gramma, inside her old house that did not feel like her old house at all.

When they spoke, their voices bounced
around the empty living room.

"What about the piano?"
asked Clee.
    Simon's fingers plinked a
high note.
    "Icicles," he whispered.

"She's a grand oldie," said Gramma. "But she's too wide in the hips for an eighth-story apartment. She'd get stuck in the elevator. She's for sale and that's why we're waiting."

"Waiting?" wondered Clee. She thought about the new apartment, bulging with Gramma's things.

Simon's fist pounded a line of low notes.

"Big storm," he shouted. Outside, the snowclouds clenched and the wind ruffled the snowbanks. A pair of headlights swept into the driveway. Gramma's piano customer had arrived.

The gentleman grumbled on the porch. He grumbled about the cold, he grumbled about the roads. He grumbled about his truck. In Gramma's hallway he tugged off his boots and grumbled about his wet socks. He was still unwrapping himself as he stepped into the living room. When he saw the piano he stopped mid-grumble.

Simon ran his hands up and down the middle keys.

"Up and down, up and down," he challenged.

Gramma shooed him off the bench.

"All mine," he added.

Clee watched the gentleman look the piano over. His eyebrows gathered close to his nose, which dripped into a handkerchief. He pressed the keys to see if they bounced back nicely.

"Chipped ivory," he muttered. Gramma flushed.

Simon slithered under the piano bench and pummeled the foot pedals with gusto. The gentleman raised his eyebrows and dug his finger into a scratch in the piano's side. Gramma turned beet red.

"I cannot pay much for this piano," the gentleman went on. "It's very old and more than likely won't hold a tune."

Simon kicked at the soundboards.

"It's too upright," groaned the gentleman, "for my bad back and my short box truck."

"Upright, upright.
Uptight, uptight,"
sang Simon.

Gramma tugged Simon out from
under the piano bench. Then
she sat, smoothed her skirt, and
placed her hands on the keys.
Beneath her fingers the chipped
ivories played "Silent Night"
and "What Child Is This?" and
a wild gypsy dance that ducked
and twirled like the snowflakes
outside the window. Clee felt
Simon's hand nuzzling into hers.

Gramma's music circled in that room. It filled all the empty corners. It tied Simon to Clee and Clee to Gramma and Gramma to her past with a ribbon of sound.

Gramma turned to the gentleman.
"This piano is not for sale," she said quietly.

The gentleman went into
reverse. He grumbled his way
back into his wet boots, rewrapped
his woolen layers around himself,
and retreated up the snowy
driveway in his truck.

The house was very quiet.
"Where is Simon?"
Clee and Gramma asked
each other.

Outside, the dark
pressed against the
windows. They looked
in bare closets and
behind doors. No Simon!
Then a small brushing
sound came from the
direction of the three
empty boxes. Gramma
put her finger to her
mouth and unflipped
the flaps of the largest
carton. Inside was a flushed
and sleeping Simon.

On that last night in the old house Clee and Gramma slept next to Simon in his box.

The big brown piano seemed to be sleeping too.

Christmas came to Clee's house that year. It was not like Gramma's old house. It did not have a hillside tucked under a frozen lake, but its windows looked out on a snow-covered garden. It had Gramma inside it, and Clee and Simon and their parents. The house was full of the smells of cooking and Christmas tree branches.

On Christmas Eve Uncle Fishtank Hal sailed through the doorway on a cloud of snow and steam.

"Yer ship's come in," he told Gramma.

That night sleep nudged around Clee's bed but had a hard time finding her. Simon slept, and the sound of his breathing mingled with the whispering of the wind outside. Downstairs her parents and Gramma were laughing. Fishtank Hal was doing a sailor dance. Clee could hear his feet.

Beneath the tree next morning everyone found a present. Clee's favorite, a gift from Fishtank Hal, was nestled in a driftwood box.

It was a beautiful shell with the whoosh of the sea inside it.

In the midst of the unwrapping, Simon discovered one more present off to the side. Unable to fit under the tree, it wore no glossy paper. But its shiny brown paint reflected the Christmas lights and its almost-white teeth stretched in a wide side-to-side smile.

Clee lifted Simon onto the bench so he could reach the chipped ivories. Gramma slid in next to them. Together they invented a song about Christmas morning. Simon played the clumps of snow falling off the roof while Gramma played the emptiness of her old house and the fullness of her new apartment. Simon played the chatter and clatter in the kitchen while Gramma played a dance that began in the past and moved sweetly into the present.

It was a ribbon of sound, a ribbon that rose and fell and filled all the corners of Clee's house.